John Pig's
HALLOWEEN

John Pig's
HALLOWEEN

Jan L. Waldron
pictures by David McPhail

Baby's First Book Club®

Text copyright © 1998 by Jan L. Waldron
Illustrations copyright © 1998 by David McPhail

First published in the United States 1998
by Dutton Children's Books, a division of
Penguin Putnam Books for Young Children, New York
Design by Ellen M. Lucaire

Printed in Hong Kong
ISBN 1-58048-045-4
Reprinted in 2000

To David,
with love, for the pictures and more

J.L.W.

To Donna,
without whose inspiration this book would not be,
and to Laurin, the magician

D.M.

It was cool and hazy on Halloween night
The silvery moon shed a ghostly white light.
As the fog billowed in and bats flitted about,
Trick-or-treat piggies got dressed to step out.

Two of the pigs made a long flowing cape
With safety pins, thread, and some shiny black tape.
Another smeared rouge on the beaming brown face
Of a piggy whose ears were wrapped in red lace.

One of the pigs wore a huge rubber nose,
Suspenders with knickers, and blue-checkered hose.
A tiny, chic pig donned a towering chapeau,
Then finished things off with a tangerine bow.

In masks and warm jackets and long floppy shoes,
The boisterous piggies perfected their *Boo's!*
But one silent piggy, whose first name was John,
Just sat in the shadows with no costume on.

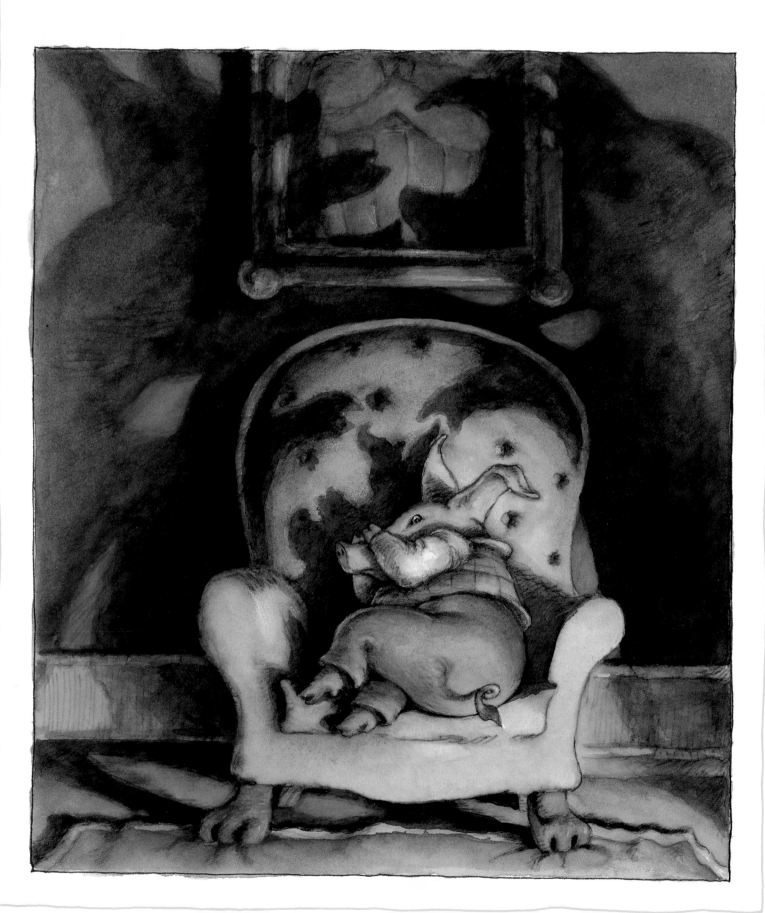

"Let's move it, let's roll, where's your bag and disguise?"

"I'm not going," John said. "Go without me, you guys."

"Not going?!" they howled. "Did we hear you right?"

"I'm tired," said John. "I'll stay home tonight."

So the gussied-up piggies all bid John adieu
As they rushed to the doorway and crowded on through.
But John wasn't tired; he was nervous and scared.
He would have dressed up and gone out if he'd dared.

When no treaters called or were even in sight,
John feared he was in for a long, lonely night.
So he pulled a fat pumpkin from deep in the pile
And carved out a face with a wide jagged smile.

Then he thought he heard grumbling outside the door
And saw wavering spirits float up through the floor.
And when a dark shadow swept past his nose,
John dove under the table—shivered and froze.

Kaboom!!! came a bang and a loud piercing yelp.
Had somebody crashed who needed his help?
He heard a long moan, then the door seemed to creak.
Who was outside? Did he dare take a peek?

When he did, what he saw was a striped yellow-eyed cat
And a small, crumpled witch in a banged-up black hat.
"What happened?" gasped John. "Are you here for a treat?"
"Of course," said the witch without skipping a beat.

"But these steps are too dark! Where's your Halloween light?"
"Just a minute," said John. "This will brighten the night."
"That's better," she said. "Now the others can see.
"So where are the goodies for Kitty and me?"

"We have long curly ribbons of red licorice
"And crystal rock candy right here in this dish."

"Yuck!" The witch scowled. "You call that a treat?
"You need savory snacks that *real* monsters can eat."

As she zoomed round the room with her broomstick and cat,
She spied leftover pumpkin and said: "Don't waste that!
"We can make a molasses-and-spice pumpkin pie.
"Salt seeds and toast them till crispy and dry.

"So put on an apron and go wash your hands.
"Then get out some bowls and a dozen round pans.
"Have you got any apples? Any cinnamon sticks?
"Find what I need, and I'll show you some tricks."

John and the witch began sifting and stirring.
She cracked the eggs as the blender was whirring.
He scooped out pumpkin and mashed it all up.
She mixed heaps of sugar and cream in a cup.

He rolled out the dough for the tarts and the pies
While the witch made witch cookies with raisins for eyes.
"Now we are cookin'," she said with a grin.
"Open the oven, we've got food to put in."

Soon more trick-or-treaters began to stop by.
They'd seen the lit pumpkin and smelled the warm pie.

"They're my pals," the witch whispered in John's little ear.
"They're loud and they're messy, but nothing to fear."
"Trick or treat!!!" howled the callers. "Bring on the fun!"
John offered them seeds, since the pies were not done.

When the Halloween goodies were ready to eat,
The noisy crowd drooled and tripped over their feet.
A man in a cape from his ears to his toes
Smeared cream on his chin and some more on his nose.
A wild woolly werewolf who howled at the moon
Slurped pie from a bowl with a big wooden spoon.

While the witch and a wizard
     slow-waltzed through the air,
A slimy green creature slipped
     right off its chair
And oozed in between dirty
     disco-ing brutes
Who had spiders with webs
     on their crusty white suits.

As this ghostly group danced and chowed down his food,
A beaming John Pig was caught up in the mood.

"I wish you could stay, and this party could last."
"Me too," gushed the witch. "This bash was a blast!

But I'm sorry to say that our gang must head back
"While the moon is still out and the sky is still black."

"There's always next year—next Halloween
"We'll come back for a visit and check out the scene."

John's housemates returned with stuffed bags and cold toes,
With Popsicle noses and lopsided bows.
"Poor John," they all sighed. "He has *really* missed out.
"He's skipped Halloween and been lonely, no doubt."

"Yikes!" said the pigs as they spotted John's pies.
They could not believe their tired pink eyes.
"Welcome home," said John Pig. "Would you care for some mousse,
"Persimmon plum pie, or my spiced apple juice?"

"Our house is so cozy, the aroma so pleasing.
"We're so tuckered out from our trick-or-treat teasing."

John offered his housemates fat muffins with cream,
Orange-striped sundaes, and pumpkin supreme.
"Look at this kitchen, there's so much to eat!
"Yummm," cooed the pigs as they downed one last treat.

John opened the pumpkin and blew out the light.
He covered the cakes and called it a night.

He climbed up the stairs and crawled into bed
With visions of goblins and ghosts in his head.

In the dark, he slept soundly, no longer afraid,
And dreamed of the many new friends that he'd made.